Belle
the Birthday
Fairy

To Josie and Lucy, with love
Special thanks to Rachel Elliot

No part of this work may be reproduced, stored in a retrieval system,
or transmitted in any form or by any means, electronic, mechanical,
photocopying, recording, or otherwise, without written permission of the
publisher. For information regarding permission, write to
Rainbow Magic Limited, c/o HIT Entertainment,
830 South Greenville Avenue, Allen, TX 75002-3320.

ISBN 978-0-545-27054-0

12 11 10 9 8   14 15 16/0

Printed in the U.S.A.   40
First Scholastic printing, January 2012

Belle

the Birthday Fairy

by Daisy Meadows

SCHOLASTIC INC.

New York Toronto London Auckland
Sydney Mexico City New Delhi Hong Kong

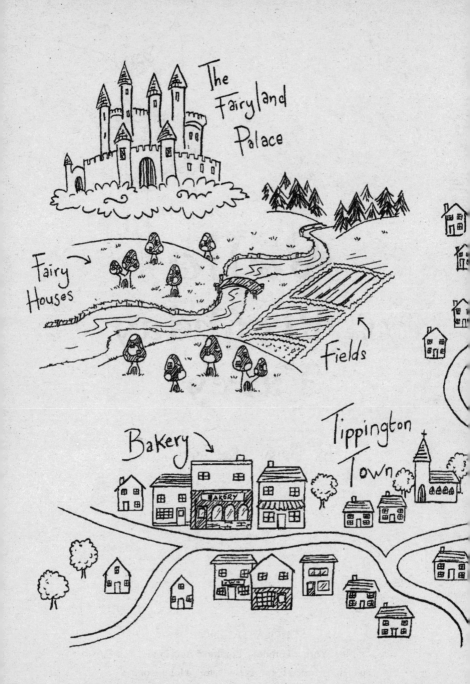

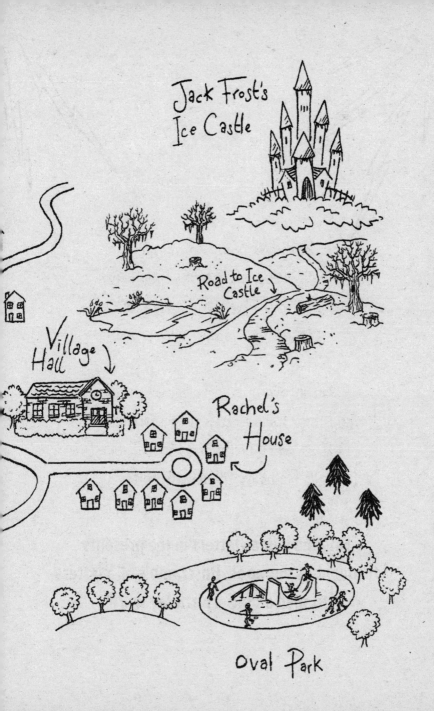

Birthdays come to everyone,
But getting older's not much fun!
Make birthday boys and girls feel bad—
Make them miserable and sad!

Banish presents, cakes, and candles!
Turn their parties into scandals.
This year's birthday treat will be:
All birthdays filled with misery!

**Find the hidden letters in the presents
throughout this book. Unscramble all 5 letters
to spell a special birthday word!**

The Birthday Book

Contents

Parties in Peril!

"I can't wait to see Mom's face when she arrives at her surprise birthday party!" Rachel Walker said with a little skip of excitement.

"Yes, she'll be so amazed when she realizes that you and your dad arranged it all!" replied her best friend, Kirsty Tate, swinging her rollerskates happily.

Kirsty was staying at Rachel's house in Tippington during school break. Rachel's mom thought that Kirsty was just there for a visit, but she was also there to attend Mrs. Walker's surprise party!

"Everything's ready," said Rachel, counting things off on her fingers. "The food, the music, the decorations for the village hall . . ."

"What about the cake?" Kirsty asked.

"Dad ordered that from the bakery," said Rachel with a smile. "He's not very good at baking, and he wanted it to be perfect!"

The friends were on their way to the local park to go rollerskating. As they passed the village hall where Mrs.

Walker's party was going to be, Rachel squeezed Kirsty's hand.

"Let's just quickly look inside," she said. "I want to show you where I'm planning to put all the decorations on the day of the party."

"Ooh, yes!" said Kirsty eagerly. "I can't wait to help you decorate the hall and lay out the food."

They peeked in the door—and their

mouths fell open in astonishment. A group
of boys and girls were there in their best
party outfits, but no one seemed to be
having a good time. The guests were
talking in low voices. They all looked
upset! Some of the parents were kneeling
on the floor, cleaning up squished cakes
and spilled drinks. A box of decorations
sat untouched by the window. There was
a stereo on the stage, but it was making

a strange whining sound and there was smoke coming out of the top.

A little girl was standing by the door with her head down. She was wearing a pretty pink dress with a white sash, but she looked very sad.

"Hello," said Rachel. "Is this your party?"

The little girl nodded her head. Her big blue eyes filled with tears.

"Everything's going wrong!" she sobbed. "Half of the guests forgot my birthday party and didn't show up. The food tables collapsed and squished my birthday cake. None of the decorations would stay up on the walls. Now the stereo is broken, so we can't even dance." Kirsty put her arm around the little girl's shaking shoulders. She didn't know what to say.

The girl's mom hurried over to them.

"I'm sorry, Maya, but Dad can't fix the stereo. We're going to have to move the party home."

"But we can't fit everyone in our house," said Maya, looking miserable.

"I know, but we have no choice," said her mom sadly. "You can pick ten friends to bring with you. Everyone else will just have to go home."

Trying not to cry again, Maya walked off with her mom. Rachel and Kirsty left and headed toward the park.

"I feel so bad for Maya," said Rachel. "It's really unlucky that all those things went wrong."

When they got to the park, they sat down to put on their rollerskates. They were both upset about the little girl's birthday being ruined!

"If only one of the Party Fairies had been here," Kirsty said with a sigh. "I'm sure they could have done something."

Rachel and Kirsty were good friends with the fairies, and had often helped them outwit mean Jack Frost and his mischievous goblins.

The girls stood up, wobbled a little, and held onto each other for balance. For a

moment, they forgot about the ruined party.

"It's been ages since you and I went rollerskating!" Rachel giggled. "I hope I can still remember how to skate without falling over!"

A New Fairy Friend

Rachel and Kirsty had only been rollerskating for a few minutes when a group of older boys walked by carrying skateboards. They all looked annoyed. Rachel spotted a boy who lived on her street in the group.

"Hi, Sam!" she called. "Have you guys been skateboarding on the park ramp?"

"Only for about five minutes," said Sam. "It's Oliver's birthday, so we were planning a whole day of skateboarding. But the ramp collapsed and the park worker sent us home. It's the only ramp in Tippington, so Oliver's birthday plans are ruined."

"That's so unlucky!" said Rachel. "Two birthdays ruined in one day!"

Kirsty frowned as the boys walked away.

"It's more than unlucky," she said. "It's too much of a coincidence."

"You're right, Kirsty!" said a musical voice behind them.

The girls whirled around in surprise. The tall hedge behind them was sparkling with colored lights. Sitting cross-legged on one of the leaves was a tiny fairy! She had long brown hair pulled back on one side with a purple flower. She was wearing a pretty purple minidress with sparkly gold ballet flats.

"Hi, girls," she said with a friendly smile. "I'm Belle the Birthday Fairy!"

"Hi, Belle!" said Rachel and Kirsty, stepping closer to the hedge so that other people wouldn't be able to see the little fairy.

"Is everything OK?" Kirsty asked. "We've seen two birthdays go wrong already this morning."

Belle's smile faded and she nodded sadly.

"King Oberon and Queen Titania sent me to ask for your help," she said anxiously. "There's no time to lose. Jack Frost has stolen the magic birthday charms!"

"What are the birthday charms?" Rachel asked in alarm.

"The birthday charms make sure that birthdays go smoothly in Fairyland and the human world," Belle explained. "Now that Jack Frost has hidden them somewhere, birthdays everywhere are going horribly wrong!"

Rachel's hand flew to her mouth.

"Oh, no!" she cried. "That means Mom's special surprise party on Saturday could be ruined!"

"Can you help me?" asked Belle. "Will you come with me to Fairyland and search for clues that might lead us to the birthday charms?"

"Of course!" cried Rachel and Kirsty together.

Belle fluttered above them and waved her wand. A burst of purple and gold fairy dust swirled out of the wand's tip and showered down on the girls. They felt themselves shrinking to the same size as Belle. Beautiful wings appeared on their backs, and Rachel and Kirsty fluttered them in delight. It was a wonderful feeling!

Belle waved her wand again. This time, the multicolored sparkles spun around them in a dizzying circle.

"It's like a merry-go-round!" Kirsty

gasped, tightly squeezing her best friend's hand.

A few moments later, the colorful blur faded away—and the girls were flying over Fairyland!

Goblin Intruders

"I thought we could start by flying over Fairyland and looking for clues," said Belle.

"So, what are the birthday charms?" asked Kirsty, as they fluttered above the emerald-green hills and tiny toadstool houses. "What exactly are we looking for?"

"There are three magic birthday charms," said Belle. "There's the birthday book, the birthday candle, and the birthday present. The birthday book lists the birthdays of everyone in both the human world and Fairyland. Without it, nobody knows when *anyone's* birthday is!"

"No wonder half of Maya's guests didn't show up today," said Rachel thoughtfully.

"The birthday candle makes all birthday cakes delicious and grants birthday wishes," Belle went on. "And the birthday

present makes sure that everyone receives
the perfect birthday gift."

"Oh my goodness!" said Kirsty.
"Without those charms, nobody will
ever have a happy birthday again!"

"I think that's why Jack Frost stole
them," Belle said, nodding. "You see, it's
his birthday soon, and he's feeling really
miserable about his age."

"So he wants everyone else to be
miserable, too?" Rachel guessed. "How
mean!"

"He doesn't want anyone to find out
when his birthday is—not even the
goblins," said Belle. "But without
the magic birthday book, we won't
know when *anyone's*
birthday is!"

The three fairies
flew along, scanning
the land below.
They were directly
over the glittering
towers of the
magical Fairyland
Palace when Kirsty gave
a cry and pointed down.

"Look!" she exclaimed.

Far below, they could see three goblins
scrambling up a ladder and climbing over
the back wall of the palace!

"I'm sure they're up to no good!" said Belle. "Come on. Let's find out what's happening!"

Rachel, Kirsty, and Belle zoomed after the goblins as they crept through a back door of the palace. The fairies followed, turning a corner to see the goblins tiptoeing into the Palace Library.

"I'm going to give those goblins a piece of my mind!" exclaimed Belle. "How dare they sneak into the palace?"

She surged forward, her cheeks pink

with indignation. Kirsty grabbed her arm and stopped her.

"Wait!" she whispered. "What if this has something to do with the birthday charms? Let's creep in and listen to what they're saying— it might give us a clue." Belle nodded, so the three fairies slipped silently into the warm, cozy library. The high walls were lined with books, some of them sparkling with magic. In the middle of the room were six squishy armchairs. Beside each armchair was a round wooden table with a glowing lamp on top of it.

"I don't think the goblins are here
to read quietly," whispered Rachel
as they ducked behind an armchair.
"Look!"

The goblins were pulling books off the shelves, row after row, and throwing them on the floor.

"Did you find it?" hissed the tallest goblin to the others.

"Not yet!" they replied.

"Well, hurry up!" the tall goblin told them. "If we can't find the birthday

book, we won't know when Jack Frost's birthday is—and we won't be able to plan his surprise party!"

Rachel, Kirsty, and Belle stared at each other in amazement. The magic birthday

book was hidden here in the Palace Library!

"It sounds like the goblins want to find the birthday book as much as we do," Kirsty whispered. "Let's try and convince them to help us!"

Belle looked doubtful.

"The goblins are never very helpful," she said.

"I think it's worth a try," said Rachel. "After all, they're disobeying Jack Frost by being here," she pointed out. "He doesn't want them to find the birthday book, so they must have a good reason for ignoring his orders. I think we should try to find out what it is!"

"Besides, it might take the three of us a long time to find the birthday book ourselves," Kirsty agreed, looking at all the books that lined the walls. "We could use the goblins' help searching for it."

Belle agreed, so they stepped out from behind the armchair and walked toward the goblins, who were still busily throwing books onto the floor. The girls tiptoed up behind them as quietly as they could. . . .

Birthday Book Hunt

"It was a good idea for Jack Frost to hide the birthday book here, wasn't it?" said Rachel in a loud voice.

The goblins spun around in surprise.

"We would never have thought of looking here if it hadn't been for you goblins," Belle agreed. "We should thank you!"

"Jack Frost knew that you silly fairies would never think to look under your

own noses!" said the smallest goblin, sticking out his tongue. "Leave us alone!"

"Don't be so rude!" said Belle. "We want to help you."

"No way!" squeaked the goblins together.

"Listen to me, goblins," said Kirsty in a friendly voice. "We overheard what you said about throwing a surprise party for Jack Frost. You need that book as much as we do. How about making a deal with us?"

"What sort of deal?" asked the tallest goblin suspiciously.

"You snuck into the palace, and that's not allowed," said Kirsty. "We should really tell you to leave right away. So here's the deal," she continued. "We'll let you stay and look up Jack Frost's birthday in the birthday book, if you promise to return the book to Belle when you're done."

The goblins gathered into a little

huddle. The girls could hear them arguing in loud whispers. But after a few minutes, they turned around and nodded.

"It's a deal!" they said in unison. Then the great birthday book hunt began! The goblins had no idea where in the library Jack Frost had hidden the book. The goblins searched the lower shelves, and the girls flew up to search the shelves that the goblins couldn't reach.

The hunt went on and on. Rachel's arms were aching from pulling out each heavy book to check it, and Kirsty's

wings were getting tired from hovering in
one position for
so long. Belle
kept flitting
down to the
lower shelves
to clean up
the books
that the
goblins were
throwing onto
the floor.

Outside the tall
library windows, the sun began to set.
It was getting late, and they still hadn't
found the magic birthday book!

"Are you absolutely sure that he hid it
in here?" Kirsty asked as she reached the
end of another row of books.

"Positive," said the middle goblin, wiping a few beads of sweat off his brow. "He said, 'Those pesky fairies will never guess that I've hidden the book in the Palace Library. I hope it makes them feel really uncomfortable!'"

"That's a strange thing to say," said Kirsty, fluttering to the ground to give her wings a rest.

Rachel flew down to join her. "Maybe we're looking in the wrong place," she said thoughtfully. "After all, Jack Frost didn't say that he had hidden the book on the shelves. He said that he wanted to make the fairies *uncomfortable*."

They all thought hard for a moment, and then Kirsty's eyes began to sparkle.

"What if that's exactly what he

meant?" she said. "What if it's in one of
the armchairs?"

Everyone stared at each other for a
minute, and then each of them rushed to
one of the six armchairs. They pulled up
the seat cushions and the smallest goblin
gave a yell of triumph.

"I've got it!"

Discoveries!

The little goblin waved a shining book above his head, but he didn't have a very good grip on it. The book flew through the air and landed safely in Belle's arms.

"The birthday book!" she cried in delight.

Rachel, Kirsty, and the three goblins eagerly gathered around Belle. The

birthday book was bound in gold, and
when Belle opened it a puff of colorful
fairy dust covered them all in sparkles.

"Look up Jack Frost's birthday!"
cried the tallest goblin. "You
promised!"

"A fairy always keeps
her promises," said Belle
calmly.

She turned the
shimmering pages
of the book. Hundreds
of thousands of names
were written there in
tiny golden letters!

"There's my mom!"
cried Rachel, pointing out
Mrs. Walker's name as the
page turned.

"There's Jack Frost!" exclaimed the goblins all at the same time.

"Oh my goodness!" said Rachel, her eyes opening wide. "Mom's birthday is on exactly the same day as Jack Frost's!"

The goblins were delighted to have gotten the information they came for. They ran home as fast as they could, promising that they would never sneak into the palace uninvited ever again.

Belle hugged the birthday book to her chest and gave the girls a big smile.

"I can't thank you enough for helping

me find this!" she
said. "If it
hadn't been
for you I
would have
thrown those
three goblins
out of the
palace. Then
I never would have
found out why they were here."

"I'm so glad we could help," said Kirsty
warmly. "Does this mean that birthdays
go back to normal now?"

"I'm afraid not," said Belle, her smile
fading. "People will remember the dates
of birthdays, but without the magic
birthday candle and birthday present,

things will keep going wrong."

"Then we'll just have to make sure that we find the other two birthday charms soon," said Rachel in a determined voice. "I'm not going to let Jack Frost ruin birthdays for everyone. I'm *definitely* not going to let him ruin my mom's surprise party!"

"I agree," said Kirsty. "Let's get started right away!"

But Belle shook her head.

"I have to return the birthday book to the present-wrapping room now. That's where it's normally kept," she said.

"Besides, look outside!"

Kirsty and Rachel turned
to the library
window. In all
the excitement,
they hadn't
noticed that
night had fallen
in Fairyland. They
could see the stars twinkling and the
moon glowing.

"It's almost my bedtime!" said Belle,
stifling a yawn. "And it's time for you two
to return to the human world."

"Will we see you again soon, so we can
search for the other birthday charms?"
Kirsty asked.

"Of course," said Belle with a smile.
"Good-bye, girls — for now!"

She flicked her wand, and there was
a whoosh of colorful sparkles. The girls
both closed their eyes.

When Kirsty and Rachel opened their
eyes again, they were standing next to
the hedge in the park, and the sun was

shining. In the distance they could see
Oliver and his friends walking away with
their skateboards under their arms.

"No time has passed at all," said
Rachel with a grin. "Oh, Kirsty, I love
magic!"

"Me, too!" said Kirsty, hugging

her friend. "Come on, let's do some rollerskating. Keep your eyes peeled for clues. Jack Frost could have hidden the other two birthday charms anywhere — and that includes the human world!"

The Birthday Candle

Contents

Cake Catastrophe

"I hope it stops raining in time for
Mom's surprise birthday party on
Saturday," said Rachel as she and
Kirsty hurried along, huddling under
an umbrella.

"Me, too," Kirsty agreed. "Birthdays
are never as much fun when it's raining."

"I wonder if Jack Frost has anything to do with this rain," said Rachel.

"I don't think we can blame him," Kirsty replied with a little giggle. "It's probably just bad weather."

"I hope Belle is OK," Rachel went on. "Time's running out! We have to find her other two charms before Mom's party."

They had helped Belle the Birthday Fairy find the magic birthday book that Jack Frost had stolen, but two of Belle's birthday charms were still missing. Without them, birthdays were going wrong all over Fairyland—and in the human world, too! Rachel didn't want anyone's party to be ruined, especially her mom's.

"Let's try not to worry," said Kirsty, putting her arm around her best friend's shoulders. "Queen Titania always says that we should let the magic come to us."

"That's true," Rachel replied, her face brightening. "Ack, Kirsty, watch what you're doing with the umbrella! You just dripped water down my back!"

"Sorry!" said Kirsty, straightening the umbrella. She glanced up. "Look, we're here!"

The two girls had arrived at the bakery. Mr. Walker had sent them on a special secret mission to pick up the birthday cake he had ordered for Rachel's mom.

"This window display always makes me

hungry," said Rachel, pausing next to the glass.

"I've never seen so many yummy treats in one place!" Kirsty agreed.

The shelves in the window were filled with a dazzling choice of cakes and pastries. There were pastries covered in fruit, cheesecakes with ruby-red strawberry glaze, and cakes topped with icing and sugared almonds.

The girls leaned closer to read some of the handwritten labels.

Kirsty let out a sigh filled with longing.

"They make the best cakes in Tippington," Rachel told her. "I can't wait to have a piece of the cake they made for Mom."

"Let's go inside and see it!" said Kirsty.

Rachel stepped inside the bakery. Kirsty shook off the umbrella and followed her.

The bakery was full of wonderful smells, and Kirsty felt her stomach start to rumble. The warm scents of cake, chocolate, nuts, and cream filled the air.

"Hello," said Rachel to the plump baker behind the counter. "We've come to pick up the birthday cake for Mrs. Walker." The man's smiling face fell.

"Oh, no," he said. "I'm so sorry, but you're going to have to come back tomorrow, instead. I'm having a lot of trouble with that cake."

He pointed to the counter behind him. He had obviously been trying to frost a cake, but something was very wrong. The cake was misshapen, and the icing was sliding off. Sugared flowers were lying beside it. The baker looked at them with a worried expression.

"This is the third cake I've tried to make for Mrs. Walker," he said. "I've used the same recipe I use for all birthday cakes, but it keeps going wrong. The cake is coming out heavy and dry, and the icing won't stay put. It's a nightmare!"

Rachel's eyes filled with tears, but Kirsty tugged on her arm.

"We'll come back tomorrow," she told
the baker. "Come on, Rachel."

"Why did we leave so quickly?" asked
Rachel as they stepped outside the shop.

"Because of what I just saw out the
window!" Kirsty whispered urgently.

She pointed at three people who were
crowding under one small umbrella
and gazing at the cake display. Rachel
rubbed her eyes and did a double take.

All three of them were wearing rainboots, raincoats, and rain hats. Between the top of the boots and the bottom of the raincoats, she could see green legs.

She gasped. "They're goblins!"

Goblins in Tippington!

Rachel and Kirsty stared in amazement as the three goblins put down their umbrella and scurried into the bakery. They tracked rainwater all over the bakery floor as they splashed inside.

"What are the goblins doing in

Tippington?" Kirsty wondered out loud.

"I don't know," said Rachel, "but *we're* getting soaked! Put the umbrella up, quick!" Kirsty raised the umbrella above their heads, but as she opened it something strange happened. The inside of the

umbrella glowed with colored lights—and then Belle spiraled down the handle, waving at them!

"Belle!" exclaimed Kirsty. "Thank

goodness you're here. Three goblins just
went into the bakery!"

"I know," said Belle,
folding her arms.
"I'm sure they're
planning some
trouble. I saw them
creep out of Jack
Frost's Ice Castle at
dawn, and they were
acting suspicious, so I
followed them. I'm glad to find you girls
here. How did you know that the goblins
were coming?"

"We didn't," Rachel explained. "We just
saw them when we came to pick up the
cake for my mom's surprise party."

"Something keeps going wrong with

the cake recipe," Kirsty added. "The baker can't make it work."

Belle's face fell.

"I knew this would happen," she said with a sigh. "The magic birthday candle helps all birthday cakes to bake perfectly and grants the birthday person a wish. Until I find it, I'm afraid no birthday cakes are going to turn out well."

"Belle, could you turn us into fairies?" asked Kirsty. "We have to find out what those goblins are up to."

"Good idea!" Belle said. "But I can't do magic here in the middle of the street."

"Let's go over there," said Rachel, pointing to a little alleyway between the bakery and the store next door.

The girls hurried down the alley and stopped when they were sure that no one

could see them from the street. Then Belle
waved her wand. A
flurry of gold and
purple fairy dust
twinkled around
the girls. It
was like
being caught
in a storm
of sequins!
They giggled
happily as the
fairy dust
settled. They
had shrunk down
to the same size as Belle, and their
gauzy wings were glistening in all
different colors.

"Let's follow those goblins and find out

what they're planning!" said Belle.

She zipped back up the alley with
Rachel and Kirsty fluttering close behind.
The bakery door was open, and all three
of them slipped in through the crack.

"Let's watch from the top of that
display cabinet," said Rachel, pointing
to a shelf. "No one will see us up there."

They fluttered up to the highest shelf
and sat on the edge. They could see the
baker bringing out cake after cake to
show the goblins. What were they up to?

"These just aren't good enough!"
squawked the tallest goblin.

"What a bunch of garbage!" squeaked
the smallest goblin.

They were causing trouble already!

Kitchen Chaos

The baker had brought out all his
most elaborate cakes and lined them
up in front of the goblins. They weren't
birthday cakes, so he hadn't had any
trouble making them.

"Boring!" shouted the middle goblin,
poking his bony finger into the first cake.

"Boring! Boring! Boring!" the other two yelled, poking their fingers into all the beautiful cakes in front of them.

"But this is my best selection!" cried the poor baker.

"Ha!" snorted the tallest goblin. "We're from the Cake Standards Board, and I'm telling you that these are terrible cakes! We'll shut this bakery down unless you start making better ones!"

The baker rubbed his forehead, looking upset.

"The Cake Standards Board?" he repeated. "But I've never heard—"

"We could make better cakes than this

standing on our heads, with our eyes shut!" yelled the middle goblin.

"Get out!" screeched the smallest goblin. "Come back in an hour and you'll see a truly magnificent cake!"

"I guess I *could* take my lunch break now," the baker stammered. "It's been a tough morning. . . ."

"Go! Go! GO!" cried the middle goblin, pressing the baker's umbrella into his hands and shoving him toward the door.

The doorbell jangled as the baker left. The goblins locked the door behind him, snickering.

"Those nasty goblins!" cried Rachel, who had been watching in shock. "How could they be so awful to that nice baker?"

"And *why*?" Kirsty added. "What do they want?"

"Let's find out!" said Belle, fluttering into the air. "Look—they're heading into the kitchen at the back of the store!"

The three girls flew through the colorful curtain that separated the store from the kitchen.

"Oh!" Belle gasped.

Suddenly, they were enveloped in a blinding white cloud!

"What is this?" Kirsty coughed, twirling around and trying to see what had happened.

"It's going in my mouth!" Rachel cried. "It's . . . it's . . . flour!"

"Fly upward!" said Belle, coughing as she breathed in the flour dust. "As fast as you can!"

The three girls zoomed toward the ceiling, and their heads broke out of the floury cloud.

As the flour began to settle, they saw
that the three goblins were running
around the kitchen. They had pulled off
their enormous rain hats and raincoats.
The tallest goblin had a chef's hat
perched on his head, and the smallest was
wearing a striped apron. The middle one
seemed jealous, and kept trying to steal
the others' outfits.

The goblins had knocked over a huge bag of flour, which had caused the cloud. The floor and the counter were smeared with broken eggs, dotted with spilled raisins, and dusted with sugar.

"Oh, no!" Kirsty exclaimed. "They're wrecking the kitchen. By the time the baker gets back, everything will be ruined!"

"We have to stop them," said Rachel with a determined expression on her face.

"Wait a minute," said Belle. "I don't think they're here just to make trouble. Look! I think they're actually trying to make a cake!"

The goblins had opened a cookbook,  and were stirring lots of ingredients into a large mixing bowl. "Stop pushing me!" squawked the goblin in the chef's hat. He elbowed the goblin in the apron and broke an egg over his head.

"It's my turn to stir!" wailed the middle goblin.

"Oh, be quiet and go get the candle!" the tallest goblin snapped.

The middle goblin pouted. He stomped over to the pile of rain hats and raincoats, and felt in the pockets. Then he pulled out a beautiful cake candle with a magic flame. It was a shimmering purple color, and glittered in the light.

Belle went pale.

"Girls, that's *it*!" she said quietly. "*That's* my magic birthday candle!"

Trapped!

As Rachel, Kirsty, and Belle stared at the
birthday candle in excitement, the other
two goblins were still arguing.

"I'm the one with the chef's hat, so I'm
in charge!" said the tallest goblin, shaking
flour into the mixing bowl.

"Oh, yeah?" snarled the one in the
apron. "You can't be in charge—you

don't even know how to read a recipe!"
He jabbed a green finger at the long
cookbook. "That says 'add *sugar*', not 'add
flour', you fool!"

"Who are you calling a fool?" shrieked
the other.

They rolled across the bakery floor,
wrestling, and crashed into the shelves.
A colorful waterfall of cake decorations,
ribbons, cake stands, and candle holders
rained down on them.

As the other goblins tumbled around
the floor, the middle goblin
continued to follow the
recipe. Rachel saw him
add a large
spoonful of
chili powder
to the mixture
and stir it in.

"That cake is
going to taste horrible!" she said to
Kirsty. "They haven't even broken the
eggs properly—I can see pieces of shell
in there."

The goblin started to pour the mixture
into a cake pan, but he needed both
hands, so he put the candle down on the
counter.

"Now's our chance!" Rachel whispered.

"I could fly down and pick up the candle before he notices!"

"It's too dangerous!" Belle whispered. "The candle is right next to him. He'll catch you!"

Rachel gulped. She knew that it was dangerous, but she couldn't stand the thought of her mom's birthday cake being ruined because of Jack Frost and the goblins.

"I've got to try," she said.

CRASH! BANG!

The other goblins were still fighting. At that moment, the middle

84

goblin turned to put the cake pan in the
oven. Rachel flew down to the counter as
fast as her wings could flutter, and
Belle and Kirsty both held
their breaths. Could she
grab the candle before
the goblin turned
around again?
Rachel reached the
candle and put her
arms under it, but it
was too heavy!
She couldn't lift herself
and the candle into
the air—and the
goblin was turning around!
Kirsty and Belle darted down to
help Rachel. But before they could
reach her, the goblin gave a yell of alarm.

"It's one of those pesky fairies!"

He grabbed a strainer and brought it crashing upside down on top of Rachel. She was trapped!

The other goblins dashed over to the counter. They were covered in egg, flour, and broken cake decorations, but they grinned when they saw Rachel hammering against the side of the strainer.

"Let me out!" she cried.

"Look, there are more of them!" yelped the middle goblin, pointing to where Kirsty and Belle were hovering in the air.

"Aha!" cried the smallest goblin, dancing around and sticking out his tongue at them. "We caught a fairy! We caught a fairy!"

Belle put her hands on her hips.

"Goblins, give me the candle and let Rachel go right now!" she said in a loud voice.

"No way!" retorted the tallest goblin.

Kirsty frowned. She thought about the

goblins creeping out of Jack Frost's Ice Castle.

"You're the same goblins who came looking for the birthday book, aren't you?" she said, thinking quickly. "Does Jack Frost know you're here?"

All three goblins went pale green.

"You're not going to tell him, are you?" asked the smallest goblin in a trembling voice.

The middle goblin began to sweat. "Oh, no — you can't!"

Kirsty and Belle exchanged confused glances. Why were the goblins causing trouble without orders from Jack Frost?

A Deal is Made

"Don't tell Jack Frost!" said the tallest goblin. "We want it to be a surprise!"

"This cake is for Jack Frost?" Rachel asked.

"Of course!" said the middle goblin. "We couldn't make it in the Ice Castle without him noticing."

"Now go away!" the smallest goblin squeaked.

"We're not leaving without Rachel and the birthday candle," Belle declared.

"That's our candle!" snapped the tallest goblin. "We found it next to Jack Frost's throne. Now it's ours, and we're keeping it!"

"They don't know that it's a magic  candle," Kirsty whispered quietly to Belle. "They just thought it would look good on the cake! They might give it to us in exchange for something better."

"What are you whispering about?" demanded the tallest goblin.

"We were just talking about the cake you made for Jack Frost's surprise party," Kirsty said. "Without magic, it will take

hours to bake. The baker will be back soon, and he won't be happy with the mess you've made. But if you agree to help us, Belle can make your cake cook faster, and then you can head back to the Ice Castle!"

The goblins made faces at the idea of helping the fairies again. Kirsty couldn't help hoping that their impatience would get the better of them.

"If we agree, we could be back at the castle in time for lunch!" the tallest goblin whispered to the others.

That did it! The greedy goblins nodded in agreement, and Kirsty smiled with relief. Belle waved her wand, and a jet of gold and purple sparkles hit the oven. The

door swung open— and the finished cake floated out and landed on the table in front of the goblins! Everyone stared at it open-mouthed.

"It's horrible!" said Kirsty.

"It's spectacular!" the goblins cried.

The cake was gray and formed sharp spikes where pieces of eggshell were sticking out. It was misshapen and ugly . . . but it was *perfect* for Jack Frost.

"It could look even better with icing and decorations," said Kirsty, winking at Belle.

"Yes!" cried the goblins, clapping their hands and dancing around the kitchen in excitement. "Make it better! Make it better!"

"I'll finish the cake for you—in exchange for two things," said Belle. "Let Rachel go, and give me the candle."

"Done!" the middle goblin declared. He lifted the strainer and Rachel flew up to join Kirsty and Belle.

"Thank you, Belle!" She smiled, stretching out her wings. Then Belle flew down to the birthday candle. She picked it up, shrank it to its fairy size, and swept her wand over the cake.

Ribbons of blue and silver fairy dust

began to curl around it. In a sparkle of magic, the cake was transformed into Jack Frost's face, covered with silver-blue

icing and topped with large candles. Belle had even written HAPPY BIRTHDAY in silver balls on the side. "I'll carry it!" shouted the smallest goblin, taking off his apron and lunging for the cake.

"No, *I'll* carry it—you're too clumsy!" yelled the middle goblin, picking up the cake and balancing it above his head.

He raced to the door, closely followed
by the other two goblins, who were still
complaining loudly.

"They didn't even say thank you!" said Kirsty, shaking her head at their rudeness.

"Never mind that," Belle replied, grinning. "I've got the magic birthday candle back!"

"And the baker will be able to make Mom's cake now," added Rachel with a happy smile.

"That poor baker!" Kirsty gasped, staring around at the mess the goblins had made.

"Don't worry!" said Belle, giving them a wink.

She flicked her wand, and the whole room shimmered. When the sparkles faded, the kitchen was gleaming and tidy, and a magnificent cake was sitting on the counter. It was decorated with pink icing

and a border of pink hearts.

"Perfect!" Rachel cried.

Then, with a wave of her wand, Belle returned Rachel and Kirsty to their human size.

"I'm taking the magic birthday candle home to Fairyland right away, but I'll see you again soon," she said. "Birthday cakes and wishes are safe—thanks to you two!"

She blew a kiss and disappeared in a flurry of fairy dust. Rachel and Kirsty smiled at each other.

"Now there's only one birthday charm missing," said Rachel. "I just hope that we can find it before Mom's party!"

"I know we can," said Kirsty, sounding confident. "After all, if we can convince those crazy goblins to help us *twice*, we can do anything!"

The Birthday Present

Contents

Party Pooper

"SURPRISE!" everyone shouted.

"Oh my goodness!" exclaimed Mrs. Walker.

Balloons flew into the air, and party poppers cracked all around the village hall, raining colored streamers over the astonished Mrs. Walker. Rachel and Kirsty each took one of her hands and led her into the center of the hall.

"What a wonderful surprise!" Mrs. Walker gasped. "How did you pull this off?"

"I couldn't have done it without these two!" Mr. Walker laughed, putting his arms around Rachel and Kirsty. The guests crowded around Mrs. Walker, hugging her and wishing her a happy birthday.

Rachel and Kirsty smiled at each other. They had spent hours decorating the hall and putting out the food. All the guests

had arrived, and then Mrs. Walker had finally walked in. She hadn't suspected a thing!

"Everything's going really well," Kirsty said in a low voice. "I was afraid that Jack Frost would ruin the party because he still has the magic birthday present."

"That reminds me — it's almost time to give Mom her special gift!" said Rachel in excitement. "Dad and I bought her a beautiful jewelry box. I can't wait to see her face when she opens it!"

"Hi, Rachel!" called two girls from

across the room. "Congratulations—
what a great party!"

"Hi, Rosie! Hi, Natalia!" Rachel
replied. "I'm glad you're having fun!"

"The cake looks beautiful!" added a
girl named Emma, whose dad had gone
to school with Mrs. Walker.

"I know—I can't wait to taste it!"
Kirsty said with a grin.

But before it was time for cake, Rachel

and Kirsty helped Mr. Walker carry their
large present to Mrs. Walker. Mr. Walker
made a little speech, and then everyone
sang "Happy Birthday."

"How exciting!" exclaimed Mrs. Walker.
She untied the big purple ribbon and
carefully tore the wrapping paper. Rachel
hopped from one foot
to another. A bubble
of excitement
rose up inside
her as Mrs.
Walker
opened the
box. . . .

"Oh," said Mrs. Walker.

"Oh, no!" groaned Rachel and Kirsty
together.

There was no beautiful jewelry box

inside—just a pair of muddy old boots!

Mr. Walker stared at the boots. He seemed to be at a loss for words. "Well . . ." said Mrs. Walker, blinking quickly, "these will be very useful for working in the garden. Thank you!"

But Rachel could see that her mom was upset. Frowning, she tugged on Kirsty's arm and led her away from the other guests.

"It's not fair!" she whispered. "I know that Mom will enjoy her party no matter what presents she gets, but she would have loved that jewelry box!"

Kirsty nodded. "It must be—"

"Are you OK, Rachel?" called her friend Antonia, who had noticed Rachel's worried expression.

"I'm fine, thanks," said Rachel, giving her a smile.

She hurried toward the door and beckoned to Kirsty to follow her. She led the way outside and around to the back of the hall, where weeds and tall bushes hid them from view.

"Ouch!" said Kirsty, as she brushed her

115

hand against a thistle. "Rachel, where are we going?"

Rachel turned with her hand on the magic locket around her neck. The king and queen of Fairyland had given each of the girls a locket.

They were full of magic fairy dust, which Rachel and Kirsty could use to

take them to Fairyland if they ever
needed help from the fairies.

"We have to help Belle find the magic
birthday present—before anything else
goes wrong at Mom's party!" Rachel
said. "Kirsty, we're off to Fairyland!"

Party
Planners

The girls opened their lockets and
sprinkled the fairy dust over their heads.
Immediately they were caught up in a
swirling cloud of sparkles. The glittering
whirl swept them off their feet and
carried them through the air.

119

Rachel and Kirsty felt themselves shrinking to fairy size. Then the sparkles faded away, and the girls were standing outside the glittering silver and pink Fairyland Palace. The large doors were wide open, and the girls could see that the entrance hall was bustling with activity. There were tables full of food, dozens of frog footmen carrying boxes and packages, and dozens of fairies flitting around.

"Oh, Rachel, look!" Kirsty exclaimed in delight. "There's

Joy the Summer Vacation Fairy! And the Rainbow Fairies are over there!"

Just then, they saw Belle hovering in a corner. Rachel and Kirsty waved at her, and she flew quickly over to them.

"Hello, girls!" she said. "I didn't expect to see you here today."

Rachel explained what had happened at her mom's party.

"What a mess!" exclaimed Belle. "Jack Frost has caused so many problems by stealing the magic birthday present. He's even ruined his own surprise party!"

"What do you mean?" Kirsty asked.

"When the king and queen heard that the goblins were planning a surprise birthday party for Jack Frost at the Ice Castle, they offered to help," Belle explained. "But there's a big problem. Follow me!"

She flitted through the palace toward the throne room. The girls followed her, waving to all their fairy friends as they went.

The king and queen were sitting on their thrones in the chamber.

Rachel and Kirsty landed before them and curtsied.

"Welcome, girls!" said Queen Titania. "It's wonderful to see you!"

"It's so nice to be here again, Your Majesty," said Rachel breathlessly. "We came because something went wrong at my mom's surprise birthday party. I'm sure it's because Jack Frost still has the magic birthday present."

"I agree," said the queen. "He's very vain, and he didn't want anyone to know that today is his birthday! But we can't prepare anything to take to his birthday party until the final charm is safely back here. That means that the goblins are up at the Ice Castle doing all the work themselves." "Things keep going wrong with the preparations," added King Oberon. "The food is burned and the decorations have gone missing." He sighed. "We have to try to get the birthday present back, but all the fairies are busy looking for the

decorations and trying to fix the food.
My magic has shown me that
the birthday present is hidden in Jack
Frost's Ice Castle, but I can't see exactly
where."

"We can go!" Rachel cried at once.
"We could get inside the Ice Castle and
hunt for the birthday present."

"Are you sure, girls?" asked the queen.
"It could be dangerous!"

The girls looked at each other. The Ice
Castle was a cold and scary place, but
they had been there before and knew
what to expect.

"We can't give up now," said Rachel.

"We want to do everything we can to
help," Kirsty insisted.

"Very well," said the queen with a
grateful smile.

"May I go with them, Your Majesties?" asked Belle.

"Certainly," said King Oberon. "But remember, the goblins can't be trusted. Look after each other!"

"We will!" said Belle, Rachel and Kirsty together.

If they could find the magic birthday present, Mrs. Walker's birthday would be a happy one and Jack Frost would get his surprise party. But goblins always guarded the towers, doors, and windows of the Ice Castle. If the girls and Belle were caught, they would be in *big* trouble!

Inside the Ice Castle

Rachel, Belle, and Kirsty gazed up at
Jack Frost's home. The castle was built
from sheets of ice, and it gleamed
menacingly. The sky was thick with dark,
heavy snow clouds. Goblins marched on
duty around the castle's pointed towers.

"How are we going to get in?" asked Rachel.

"Look!" cried Kirsty. A goblin was zooming along the road toward them on a motorcycle, pulling a large trailer. He was wearing big driving goggles and a white silk scarf. The girls darted behind a tree.

"What's in the trailer?" Rachel wondered aloud.

"I think it's party decorations!" said Kirsty.

A gray paper streamer had come loose and was dragging on the road. Just then, the goblin looked back and noticed it. He stopped the motorcycle and jumped off to pack the streamer away.

"That's our way in!" Kirsty declared in an excited whisper.

Belle, Rachel, and Kirsty flitted over to the trailer and tucked themselves under the tarp that covered it just as the goblin started up the motorcycle again.

They couldn't see anything, but they could hear the wheels of the trailer rumbling over the icy, uneven road. Then the engine was shut off and the trailer was dragged over bumpy cobblestones.

"Where are we having the party?" asked a goblin voice.

"In the Great Hall," came the reply. "Those pesky fairies haven't showed up to help, so we have to do it all ourselves! Jack Frost's presents are already in there. We'll decorate when he isn't looking."

The girls heard the goblins walk away. When their grumbles had faded into the distance, Kirsty carefully lifted the tarp.

"All clear!" she said.

They fluttered out of the trailer and looked around. They were in the castle courtyard, which had several dark hallways leading out of it.

"Let's go!" whispered Rachel. "The goblins could come back any minute!"

The three friends flew into one of
the hallways. It was narrow, cold, and
gloomy. At last, they reached a pair of tall
double doors with the words GREAT HALL
carved above them.

Suddenly, the door handles started to
turn. The girls looked around in panic.
There was nowhere to hide!

"Up!" Belle whispered urgently.

They all flew up to the ceiling and hovered there, pressing their backs against the cold roof. The doors burst open and Jack Frost stormed out. He looked up and down the hall.

"There's no one around for me to yell at!" he snarled. "Where are those goblins?"

His long, thin fingers stroked his icy chin.

"I really hate birthdays," he muttered

to himself. "So I'm going to make everyone suffer!"

He strode off, his cloak flowing behind him. As soon as he disappeared around the corner, the girls let out huge sighs of relief. They darted into the hall and  closed the doors softly behind them. Jack Frost's throne stood in the center, and long tables covered with gray tablecloths lined the room. The three friends lifted the tablecloths and peered behind curtains, but all they found were cobwebs and a few bugs. No magic birthday present!

"There's one more place we haven't looked," said Rachel.

Jack Frost's throne stood on a raised platform. The girls searched along the sides of the throne and under the cushion. Then Rachel crouched down behind the throne. There was a hollow space inside the platform, and the three friends gasped when they saw what was inside.

"Presents!" said Kirsty in a breathless voice. "These must be the goblins' gifts for Jack Frost!" The girls pulled them out one by one.

"There's something else at the back,"
said Belle, peering into the darkness.

Rachel reached in, stretching her arm
as far as it would go. At last she pulled
out a little box, wrapped in shiny pink
paper and decorated with balloons.

"It's much sparklier than the others, and
it feels as light as a feather!" said Rachel,
wondering what this present could be.

Belle's eyes were bright and shining
with excitement.

"That's because it's my magic birthday
present!" she said. "We've found it!"

A Brave Act

Suddenly, the double doors flung open and the girls heard a bunch of chattering voices. Kirsty peeked around the side of the throne.

"It's the goblins!" she exclaimed. "They're here to decorate the hall for the surprise party. Belle, can you use your magic to send us back to the palace?"

Belle waved her wand . . . but nothing happened!

"Jack Frost must have put a spell on this room," she said in a worried whisper. "It means that I can't do magic until I get outside."

"We're trapped!" Rachel exclaimed.

"If we can't return the magic birthday present to the palace, the preparations for Jack Frost's party won't work," cried Belle.

"And it's only a matter of time before the goblins spot us here," added Kirsty.

She looked at her best friend in panic, but Rachel was gazing up at the tall,

pointed windows of the Great Hall.
One of them was open slightly, but
there were three goblins standing right
underneath it.

"We can't
fly out of
there,"
said Belle.
"The
goblins
would be
close
enough to
grab us."

Rachel raised
an eyebrow. "Not if they're distracted,"
she said with a little smile.

"That's it!" Kirsty exclaimed. She
turned to Belle. "Rachel and I will create

a distraction on the other side of the hall. While the goblins are looking at us, you can fly out of the window!"

Belle looked worried.

"I don't want to leave you here," she said. "It could be dangerous. What if the goblins catch you? What if Jack Frost finds you?"

"The king and queen are coming here for the surprise party," said Rachel. "We can face anything, knowing that our friends are on their way!"

Belle hugged them both.

"I think you're both really brave," she said. "Thank you! I'll be as fast as I can!"

Rachel and Kirsty each took a deep breath. Then they held hands and flew out from behind the throne, heading toward the far end of the hall.

"Hey, goblins, over here!" shouted Kirsty.

The goblins let out howls of anger.

"It's a pair of pesky fairies!"

"Get them!

"Catch them!"

"Stop them!"

The goblins all rushed to join in the chase, and a sea of bony green fingers snatched the air near Rachel and Kirsty. Not a single goblin noticed Belle slip quietly out of the window. But Rachel and Kirsty saw her go, and they smiled at each other. Now they just had to keep out of the goblins' way until help arrived!

The two friends flitted around the hall, dodging back and forth to keep out of the goblins' clutches. One goblin jumped onto another's shoulders and tried to grab Rachel, but she did a somersault in midair. The goblin lost his balance and crashed to the floor with a yell. Another goblin bounced up and down on the throne cushion, and then launched himself through the air at Kirsty. She flew

to one side at
the last minute.
The goblin
hit the
dangling
chandelier
and hung there,
yelling for help. It was chaos!

"Just keep them busy!" Kirsty panted,
flying higher to escape an especially tall
goblin.

"My wings feel so tired." Rachel
gasped. "I'm not sure how much longer
I can—"

"WHAT IS GOING ON?" roared a
furious voice.

The girls screamed, and all the goblins
froze on the spot. Jack Frost was standing
in the doorway!

"Fairies!" Jack Frost hissed. "I know why you're here! You'll never find the magic birthday present."

"You're too late!" said Kirsty.

"Never!" he snarled. "I hid it far too well for you to find it!"

He lunged toward the throne.

"He'll find his presents!" squealed a goblin. "Stop him!"

Every single goblin hurled himself at

Jack Frost, who disappeared in a pile
of green arms and legs.

"Get off me!" his muffled voice yelled.
"I'll banish you all, you foolish goblins!"

"That would be a terrible mistake," said
the gentle voice of Queen Titania just
then. "They're only trying to give you a
happy birthday."

The fairies had arrived!

Parties Galore!

With a wave of the queen's wand, Jack
Frost's spell on the room was lifted.
The Great Hall was transformed into a
sparkling party scene! Fairies fluttered
in carrying frosted party food and
glittery snowflake decorations. The
gray tablecloths turned silvery blue,
and the ceiling shimmered with icicles.

The goblins scrambled to their feet and rushed to add their decorations to the room. Jack Frost stood up, scowling and smoothing out his beard.

"What do *you* want?" he snapped at the king and queen.

King Oberon stepped forward.

"Everyone deserves a very special birthday, including you," he said. "The goblins care about you, and they wanted you to have a wonderful party. We were happy to help."

Jack Frost's eyes opened very wide. His mouth fell open.

"Getting older is something to be

celebrated!" Queen Titania added.

Jack Frost looked too surprised to speak. Then the three goblins who had organized the party stepped proudly forward, carrying the misshapen cake. Its sharp, ugly spikes were frosted with blue-silver icing, and there were candles stuck out of it at all different angles. Silver balls spelled out HAPPY BIRTHDAY! across the bottom, and the goblins had added a gray ribbon at the base as a finishing touch. As Jack Frost stared at it, everyone started to sing.

"Happy birthday to you . . ."

Once the song ended, there was a moment of silence. Then Jack Frost leaned forward, closed his eyes, and took a deep breath. After a second, he opened his eyes and blew out all the candles.

"There's something missing from this party," he said.

"Uh-oh. I hope he's not going to do anything mean," Rachel whispered.

He turned to a few of the goblins and tapped his wand on their heads. They were instantly transformed into the Gobolicious Band!

"Hooray!" shouted the goblins.

King Oberon gave a wave of his wand and a stage appeared.

"And now, a special performance from Frosty and his Gobolicious Band!" King Oberon announced with a smile.

Jack Frost pulled some sunglasses from his pocket and stepped up to the microphone.

"Maybe birthdays aren't so bad after all," he said. "Let's rock!"

It was the best party ever held in the Ice Castle. Rachel and Kirsty danced with all their fairy friends. They even tried to dance with the goblins, but the goblins kept stepping on their toes and giggling.

As night fell, the queen waved Rachel, Kirsty, and Belle over.

"I am so grateful to you for finding the birthday charms," she said. "Thanks to you, we were able to show Jack Frost that birthdays *can* be fun."

"We were glad to help," said Rachel, hugging Belle.

"It's time for you to be getting home," said the queen with a twinkle in her eyes. "I believe you have another party to attend!"

"My mom's birthday party!" Rachel exclaimed.

Belle hugged Rachel and Kirsty good-bye. "Thank you so much for all your help!" she said.

She tapped them both on the hand with her wand, and there was a sparkling flash. When the girls looked down, each of them had a heart-shaped ring on her little finger.

"Thank you!" they cried.

As they spoke, a whirl of glittering fairy dust surrounded them. They felt themselves rising into the air and spinning as if they were dancing.

When the sparkles faded, they were standing outside the Tippington village hall.

"Let's go and find Mom!" Rachel said eagerly.

They ran back into the hall, just in time to see Mrs. Walker opening her beautiful jewelry box.

"I must have gotten the boxes mixed up!" Mr. Walker was saying. "Silly me!"

"Thank goodness," said Kirsty. "It's the perfect present!"

Rachel smiled at Kirsty and squeezed her hand.

"No gift could be better than the adventure we just had!" she said.

Don't miss any of Rachel and Kirsty's other fairy adventures! Check out this magical sneak peek of

Read on for a special sneak peek . . .

School Trip

"I feel like it's my birthday and Christmas all at once!" said Rachel Walker, bouncing up and down in her seat. "I can't believe we're actually going to a sleepover in the National Museum!"

"It makes it twice as exciting that you're here," her best friend Kirsty Tate agreed, settling down beside her. "It was so nice of the principal to let you come."

Kirsty's school had won a place in a giant sleepover, which was being held at the National Museum. Thirty kids from the school were going to the city to take part. Rachel was staying with Kirsty that weekend, so she had been allowed to join in, too.

The bus driver took his place and the engine rumbled into life. As the bus pulled out of the school parking lot, the girls waved good-bye to Kirsty's mom, who had come to see them off.

"I hope it's not spooky there at night," said a girl named Hannah, who was sitting in the seat behind Rachel. "I'm a little scared of the dark."

"Don't worry," said Kirsty with a

comforting smile. "I've been there before and it's really cool. There are tons of amazing things to do."

"I want to see the dinosaur gallery!" said Rachel, opening a bag of candy and offering some to everyone around.

"Ooh yes, and the diamond exhibition with all the sparkling gems and jewels," Kirsty added, taking a piece of chocolate and popping it into her mouth.

"The marine fossils!" said Arthur.

"The wildlife garden!" said Ali.

"The world lab!" said Dan.

Suddenly, there was a loud bang underneath their feet.

"What was that?" Hannah squealed. "Did a wheel come off?"

RAINBOW magic™

There's Magic in Every Series!

The Rainbow Fairies

The Weather Fairies

The Jewel Fairies

The Pet Fairies

The Fun Day Fairies

The Petal Fairies

The Dance Fairies

The Music Fairies

The Sports Fairies

The Party Fairies

The Ocean Fairies

The Night Fairies

The Magical Animal Fairies

Read them all!

■ SCHOLASTIC

www.scholastic.com

www.rainbowmagiconline.com

HiT entertainment

RMFAIR®